WE DEEPLY APPRECIATE OUR CUSTOMERS' FEEDBACK! IF YOU'VE HAD THE CHANCE TO TRY OUT OUR COLORING BOOK, WE'D BE GRATEFUL IF YOU COULD TAKE A MOMENT TO SHARE YOUR EXPERIENCE BY LEAVING A REVIEW ON AMAZON.

OUR COLORING BOOK IS IDEALLY SUITED FOR COLORING PENCILS AND ALCOHOL-BASED MARKERS. FOR THOSE USING WET MEDIUMS, WE RECOMMEND PLACING A SHEET OF PAPER BEHIND THE PAGES TO PREVENT ANY POTENTIAL BLEED-THROUGH.

SHARE YOUR BEAUTIFUL CREATIONS FROM OUR COLORING BOOK ON INSTAGRAM, FACEBOOK, OR TIKTOK!

#TAMAKUMOCOLORING

JOIN OUR COLORFUL COMMUNITY!

 TAMAKUMO COLORING BOOKS

 TAMAKUMO.COLORING

 TAMAKUMO.COLORING

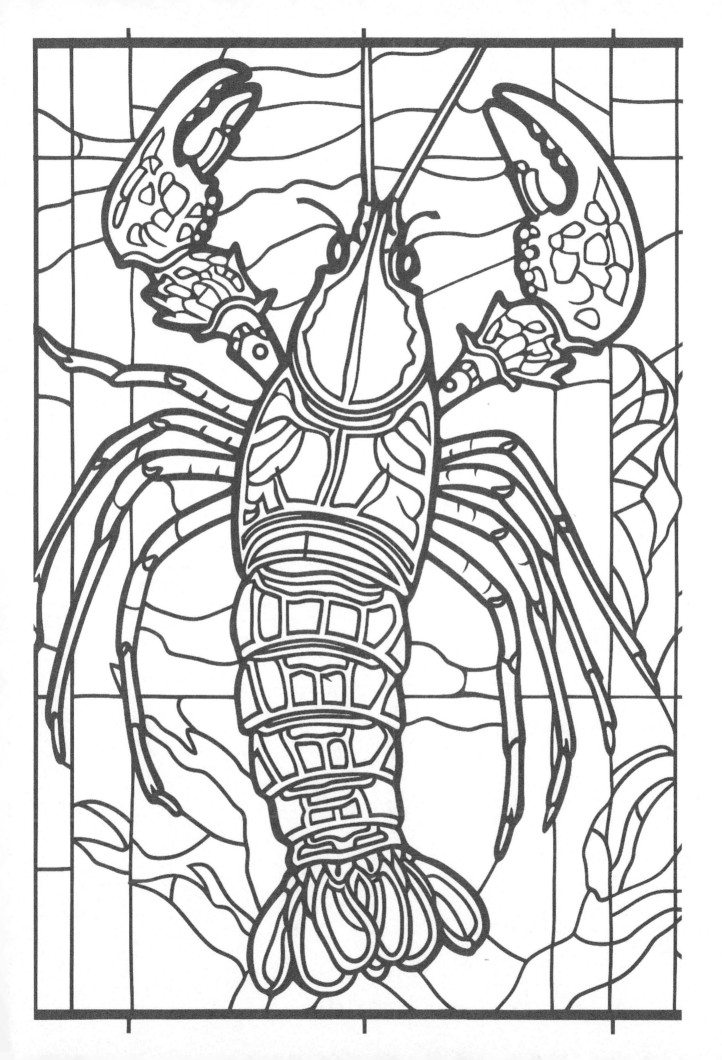

Made in United States
Orlando, FL
28 November 2024

54606083R00037